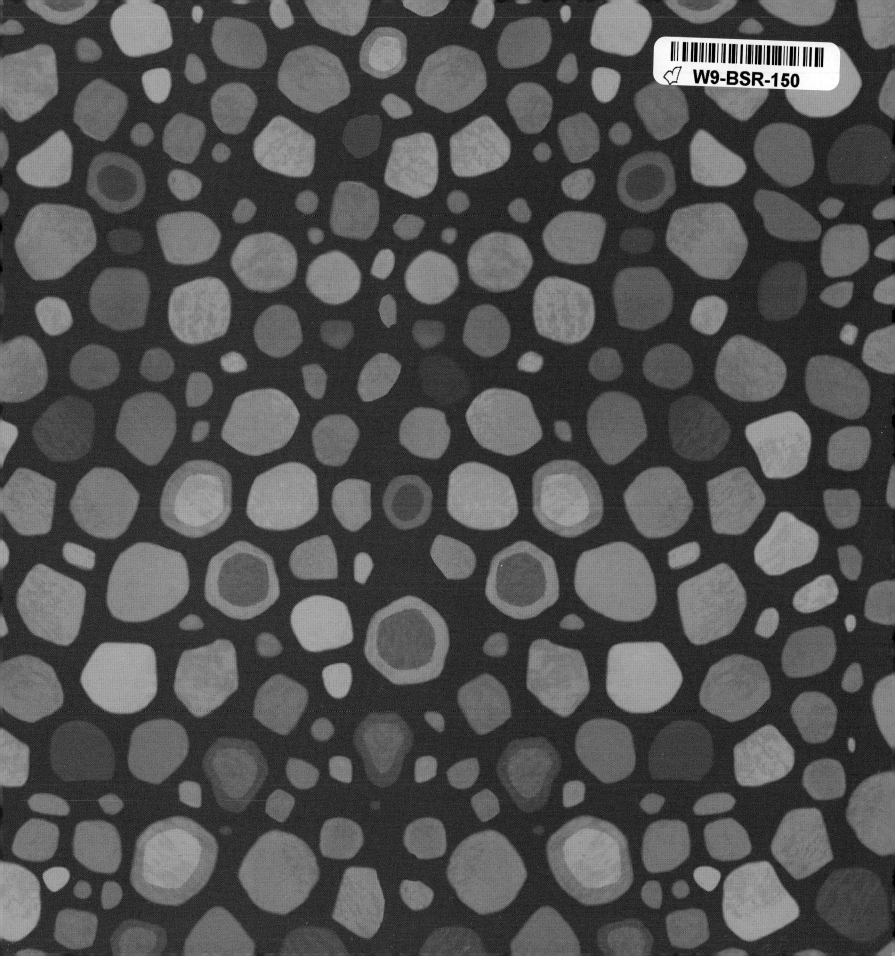

First U.S. edition 2020
Published by Templar Publishing (U.K.) 2020

Library of Congress Catalog Card Number pending
ISBN 978-1-5362-1400-0 (hardcover)
ISBN 978-1-5362-1401-7 (paperback)

21 22 23 24 TLF 10 9 8 7 6 5 4 3 2

Printed in Dongguan, Guangdong, China

This book was typeset in Kosmik and DK Black Bamboo.
The illustrations were created digitally.

Candlewick Entertainment
an imprint of
Candlewick Press
99 Dover Street
Somerville, Massachusetts 02144

visit us at www.candlewick.com

GIGANTOSAURUS™

THE LAST DRAGONFLY

CANDLEWICK
ENTERTAINMENT

Mazu and her friends were exploring deep in the prehistoric jungle when Mazu discovered the entrance to the secret cave she had been looking for. But something was standing in her way — a giant dinosaur-eating plant!

In a split second, Mazu found herself hanging upside down by her tail.

"I really don't think that plant wants to be friends with you," Tiny called.

"I'll save you!" Rocky cried.

"It's okay, Rocky!" said Mazu. "My tail doesn't taste very good. Watch this!"

Sure enough, the plant spat Mazu out, setting off a series of traps and clearing a path to the cave's entrance.

Rocky, Tiny, and Bill went down to the river as Mazu went inside the cave.

"Now to get what I came for," she said. "I know you're in here somewhere."

The little dino searched among the thick moss, hanging vines, and unusual flowers. At last she heard a fluttering sound in the corner. Her face lit up.

Mazu reached into the shadows and a beautiful yellow dragonfly hopped onto her hand.

When Mazu joined her friends by the river, they were very surprised to see that all she had found was a dragonfly.

"You know Mazu," replied Tiny. "She'll do ANYTHING for science!"

"This dragonfly isn't just ANY bug," explained Mazu. "She's the last of her kind, and she's ready to have babies. If I don't find her a safe spot to lay her eggs, she'll go EXTINCT!"

Just then, two sneaky dinosaurs appeared and snatched the dragonfly.

Did she say IT STINKS?!

It smells OK to me!

The raptors, Totor and Cror, had stolen the dragonfly, and they weren't about to return her anytime soon!

"Give me back that dragonfly!" Mazu yelled. "She's very rare!"

But the raptors leapt out of reach and waved the insect in the air to taunt the little dinosaurs.

GIVE HER BACK!

Mazu thought fast. "If you give me back that dragonfly, I'll give you something even rarer — a SCALE from GIGANTO!"

"You'd have to be the bravest dino on the planet to do that," sneered Cror.

Totor and Cror sniggered, then turned back toward the jungle. "You get us the scale," Cror shouted over her shoulder, "and you can have the dragonfly back!"

The challenge was set. Now Mazu HAD to find Gigantosaurus!

While the others searched for Giganto, Bill found something he liked better — yummy yellow honey dripping from a dinobee nest.

"I don't think Giganto's up there," said Tiny as a drip landed in Bill's mouth. "That's just a bunch of bees."

Mmmm, it's so gooey!

As they walked on they heard a strange humming noise. It got louder and louder.
Uh-oh! Bill had disturbed the . . .

DINOBEES!

The friends sprinted through the jungle, away from the swarm of bees.
Then they bumped into something big and green . . .
something with VERY large teeth . . .

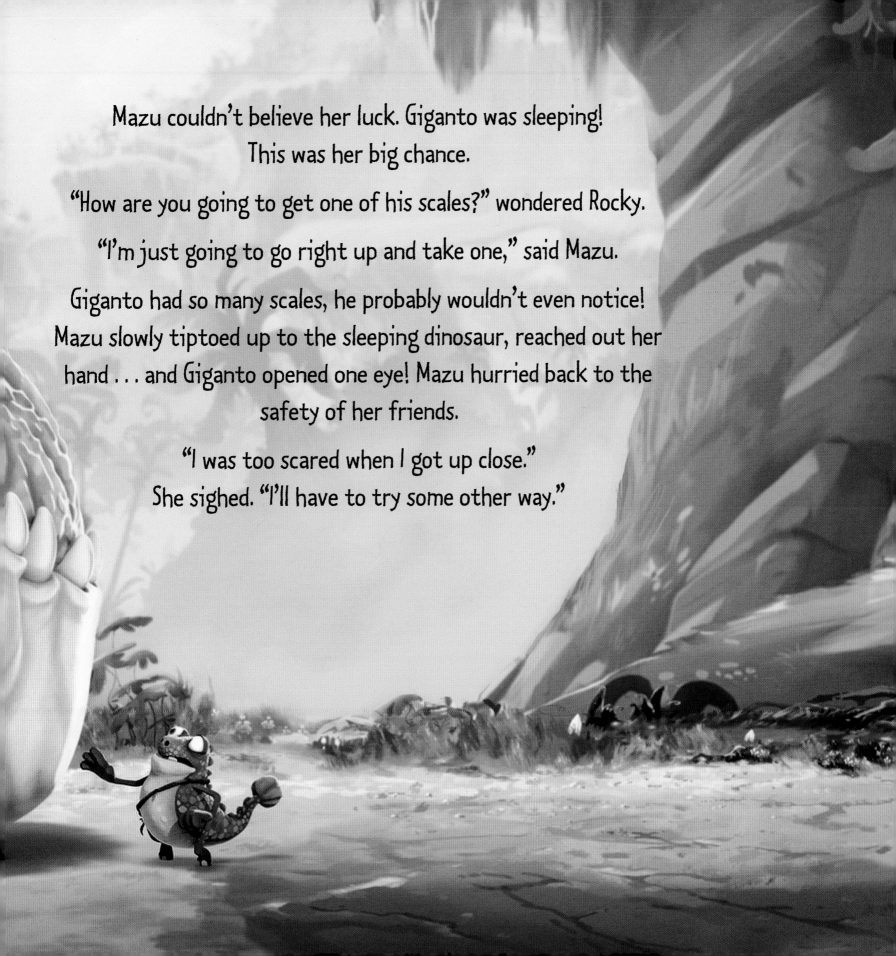

Mazu couldn't believe her luck. Giganto was sleeping!
This was her big chance.

"How are you going to get one of his scales?" wondered Rocky.

"I'm just going to go right up and take one," said Mazu.

Giganto had so many scales, he probably wouldn't even notice!
Mazu slowly tiptoed up to the sleeping dinosaur, reached out her
hand . . . and Giganto opened one eye! Mazu hurried back to the
safety of her friends.

"I was too scared when I got up close."
She sighed. "I'll have to try some other way."

Mazu thought quickly. How could she get hold of one of Giganto's scales from a distance? She spotted a hanging vine and a sharp rock and had an idea.

"I'm going to swing this vine over Giganto," she explained, tying the rock to the end of the vine. "The rock will cut the scale right off his back!"

She swung the vine around her head and practiced catching a flower.

But as she looked down at the pointy rock, Mazu realized something. "Wait . . ." she said, worried. "What if Giganto can get hurt, just like us?"

Mazu needed to find another way to get a scale from Giganto. She wasn't going to give up on her dragonfly friend.

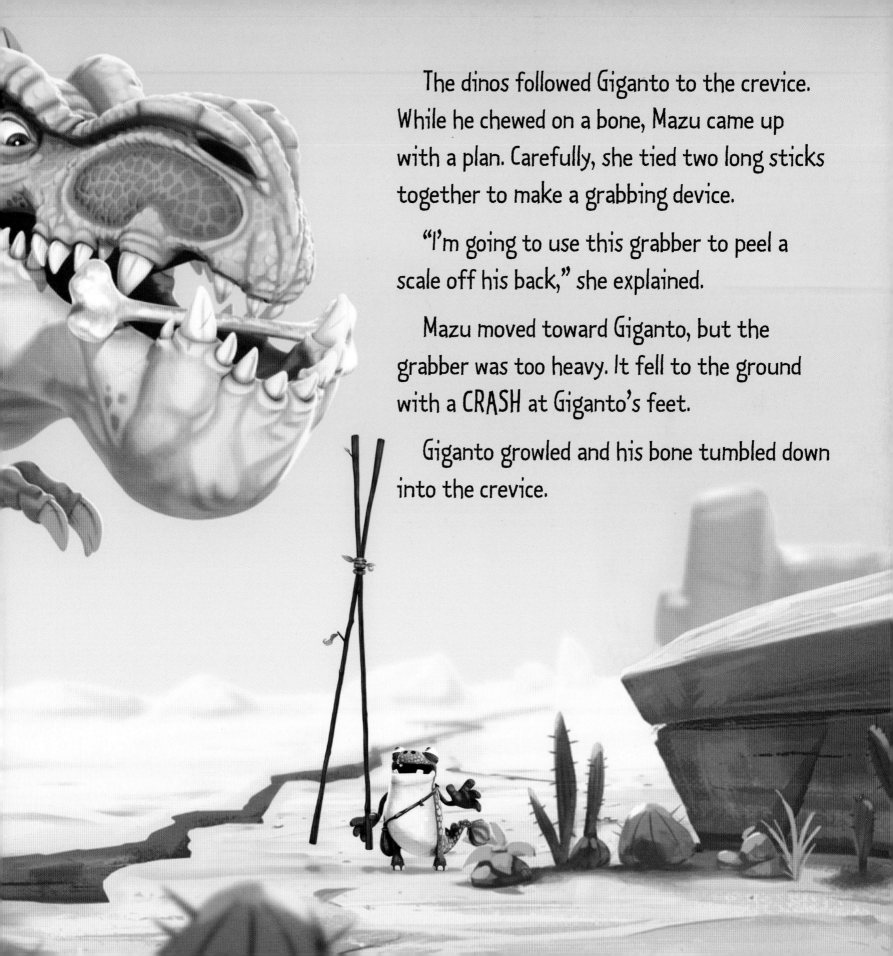

The dinos followed Giganto to the crevice. While he chewed on a bone, Mazu came up with a plan. Carefully, she tied two long sticks together to make a grabbing device.

"I'm going to use this grabber to peel a scale off his back," she explained.

Mazu moved toward Giganto, but the grabber was too heavy. It fell to the ground with a CRASH at Giganto's feet.

Giganto growled and his bone tumbled down into the crevice.

Gigantosaurus looked mad. He had lost his lunch!

"Everything I've tried has failed," Mazu groaned.

"Don't give up," urged Rocky. "You can fail a bunch of times and still succeed!"

Bill nodded. "That little dragonfly is counting on you."

Her friends were right. With fresh determination, Mazu picked up her grabber and ran back. At least she could try to save Giganto's lunch! Mazu carefully lifted the bone out and pushed it toward Giganto.

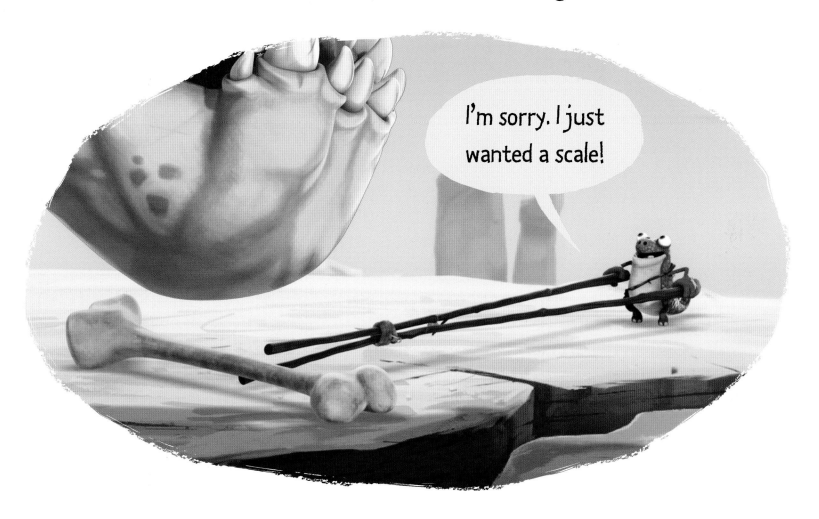

Giganto didn't look so angry anymore, and he stomped away to eat in peace. But Mazu still didn't have a Giganto scale.

"I'll NEVER get the dragonfly back!" Mazu sobbed.

Mazu didn't get upset very easily. Her friends knew she would come up with a new plan. Mazu was so smart; she just needed to use her head.

We'll show her who's smarter!

Back in the jungle, the raptors had left the dragonfly inside a cage of twigs and gone off to make more mischief.

Totor spotted a suspicious-looking vine stretched across the path.

"It's probably one of Mazu's crazy traps," he said.

The raptors jumped over the vine and landed on a loose rock that tipped upward.

"Uh-oh!" they yelled. Suddenly the pair were tied up and dangling from a tree.

Mazu leapt out from her hiding place and rushed over to free the dragonfly.
The little creature flew into the air, then settled happily on her rescuer's hand.

"You did it, Mazu!" cheered her friends. They knew she would find a way!

"I guess I didn't need Giganto's scale after all," said Mazu.
"But imagine if I HAD managed to get one. . . ."

Just then the ground began to shake. Giganto was back! He peered down at Mazu, then rubbed his back against a tree, as if he was scratching an itch. A single scale fell to the ground.

Thank you!

Later, Mazu watched proudly as the dragonfly eggs hatched.
Around her neck was a very special scale necklace.

A tiny baby dragonfly fluttered into the air. Soon there was another and another!
Mazu skipped after them happily. She had done her very best and now the
dragonfly species was saved.

"Can I wear Giganto's scale now?" begged Bill. "PLEASE?"

"Sure," said Mazu.

"ROARRRR! I'm Gigantosaurus!" growled Bill. "I'm not scared of *anything*... ARGGH!" He squealed with fright as another of the little bugs buzzed by.

"Except for a baby dragonfly!" said Tiny, giggling.

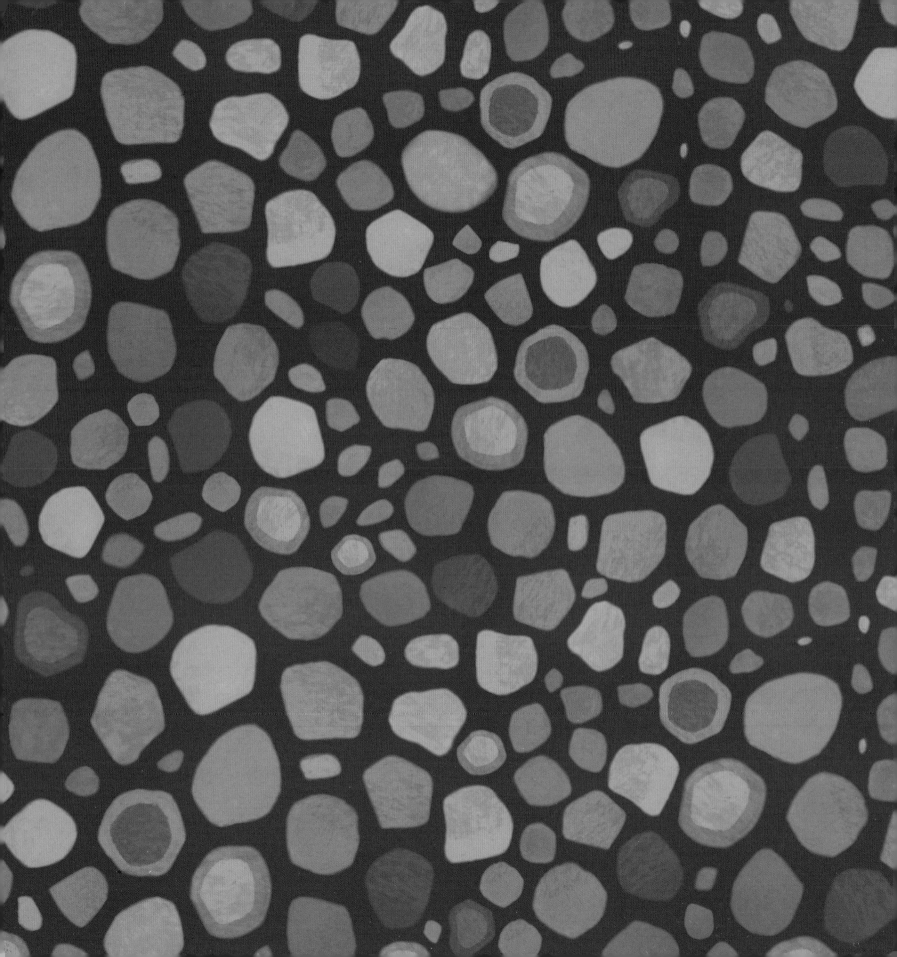